Refreshment for the Caregiver's Spirit

Loretta Woodward Veney

Copyright © 2020 by Loretta Woodward Veney

ISBN 978-1-4958-1374-0
ISBN 978-1-4958-1375-7 eBook
Library of Congress Control Number: 2017903664

Published March 2020

Dedication

I dedicate this book to Timothy MacBeth Veney, my biggest cheerleader, best friend of 36 years, soulmate and husband of almost 31 years. This book wouldn't be possible without the amazing photos he took on our many travels and adventures. Tim loved life and lived it to the fullest each and every day. He had a magnetic smile and captivating laugh and impacted the lives of everyone around him. Tim made you feel special even if you only met him once, and he made my Mom feel special on each and every visit, even after she no longer remembered who we were.

When I became an author as part of my fight against Alzheimer's disease, Tim was with me every step of the way. He packed and mailed books all around the country, and entertained folks standing in line at my book signings. Tim knew I was working on this book to lift the spirits of Caregivers, and he was thrilled that some of his favorite photos would become part of the book. I'm devastated that he died after a very short illness on July 17, 2016, but he lives on in the lives of all of us who knew and loved him. Tim, Thank you for loving me and for always holding me up! I miss you every day and will love you always!

Cover photo: Naples, Italy © Tim Veney, 2016

Introduction

Mom was very aware after her 2006 diagnosis that she had dementia, and as her condition worsened she used to always say "I don't know what I'm doing!" in the most exasperated voice you can imagine. It always hurt me to my core when she'd say that and it spurred me to continue doing whatever I can to help find a cure for this dreaded disease. As mom's condition worsened I needed inspiration on many days!

Over the years, I've been inspired by many of the photos Tim and I have taken on our travels and I began writing inspirational quotes to accompany some of my favorite photos and saved them to look at when I was having a bad day. The photos really perked mom up too, and she'd say "wow" upon seeing many of the scenic views. She was amazed that Tim and I had traveled to so many places and taken all the photos ourselves. Because we loved the photos so much, I decided to publish them in a book in the hopes that they might be uplifting for others. In honor of my mom, there's no rhyme or reason or specific order to the photos, just as there's no order in mom's brain because of her dementia.

No matter who you are caring for or what disease they have, I hope our photos and quotes in this book help to refresh your spirit!

You can conquer any
situation when you
have great support!

Watching the sun rise can change both
the landscape and your mindset.

Grand Canyon National Park, Arizona © Tim Veney, 2016

Engage your active imagination! You may even see an ice cream cone in the desert.

Red Rock Canyon, Nevada © Loretta Woodward Veney, 2016

When you view life from a positive perspective your problems are more manageable!

Mt. Rigi, Switzerland © Tim Veney, 2016

Surround yourself with people who support you no matter which way the wind blows!

Copenhagen, Denmark © Tim Veney, 2016

It takes a village to overcome mountainous obstacles! Know who in your village can be of help to you!

Jungfrau, Switzerland © Tim Veney, 2016

Wherever you are, take a minute to enjoy the view!

Mt. Rigi, Switzerland © Tim Veney, 2016

Climbing to the top is worth all the effort!

Tuscany, Italy © Loretta Woodward Veney, 2016

Spending time on a body of
water can make you feel grand!

Grand Canal Venice, Italy © Loretta Woodward Veney, 2016

Even if things look bleak
better times are right around the corner!

Santorini, Greece © Loretta Woodward Veney, 2016

Porto Santo Stefano, Italy © Tim Veney, 2016

Grab a lifeline when you need one!

Cancun, Mexico © Loretta Woodward Veney, 2016

Mt. Rainier National Park, Washington © Loretta Woodward Veney, 2016

Stand tall even if things begin
to crumble around you!

Ephesus, Turkey © Loretta Woodward Veney, 2016

Go to your place of solitude often
even if it's only in your mind!

Tuscany, Italy © Loretta Woodward Veney, 2016

18

Take a walk in your neighborhood to embrace the beauty you may be missing!

Lucerne, Switzerland © Loretta Woodward Veney, 2016

Steer carefully to avoid debris
that could throw you off your path!

Glacier Bay National Park, Alaska © Tim Veney, 2016

Driving can be freeing, even if you have no idea where you're headed!

Tuscany, Italy © Loretta Woodward Veney, 2016

Scenery that takes your breath away
can immediately renew your spirit!

Lucerne, Switzerland © Tim Veney, 2016

When the world feels as cold
as ice, sip a warm drink!

Glacier Bay National Park, Alaska © Loretta Woodward Veney, 2016

When advocating for loved ones be a giant force!

Abu Simbel, Egypt © Loretta Woodward Veney, 2016

Stunning architecture is serene!

Santorini, Greece © Tim Veney, 2016

Every step you take brings
you closer to success!

Chichen Itza, Mexico © Tim Veney, 2016

Prickly situations require immediate solutions.

Scottsdale, Arizona © Loretta Woodward Veney, 2016

27

As water washes over rocks,
peace washes over you!

Barbados, Lesser Antilles © Tim Veney, 2016

Your faith holds your foundation together even if a few pieces of you fall apart.

Glacier Bay National Park, Alaska © Tim Veney, 2016

Aswan, Egypt on the River Nile © Loretta Woodward Veney, 2016

You can conquer anything when you stand strong!

Luxor, Egypt © Loretta Woodward Veney, 2016

Copenhagen, Denmark © Tim Veney, 2016

Bright colors uplift your spirits!

History teaches us that one bad day isn't the end of the world!

Tulum, Mexico, © Loretta Woodward Veney, 2016

Take a hike to clear your mind!

Corfu, Greece © Tim Veney, 2016

Find inspirations that make
you want to jump for joy!

Milan, Italy © Loretta Woodward Veney, 2016

Patience and preparation make
it easier to reach the pinnacle!

Grand Canyon National Park West Rim, Arizona © Tim Veney, 2016

An island is the perfect antidote for stress!

St. Thomas, U.S. Virgin Islands © Loretta Woodward Veney, 2016

May your life reflect everything positive about you!

Maple Valley, Washington © Loretta Woodward Veney, 2016

Gather your strength to cross life's bridges!

Mt. Rainier National Park, Washington © Loretta Woodward Veney, 2016

Rhodes, Greece © Tim Veney, 2016

Take a seat to take care of you!

Maui, Hawaii © Loretta Woodward Veney, 2016

Mt. Rainier National Park, Washington © Loretta Woodward Veney, 2016

Instead of sitting idle, make a grand entrance into your life!

Cancun, Mexico © Loretta Woodward Veney, 2016

Shafer Trail in Moab, Utah © Loretta Woodward Veney, 2016

Porto Santo Stefano, Italy © Loretta Woodward Veney, 2016

Taking great care of everything you love can have amazing results!

Siena, Italy © Tim Veney, 2016

Slow down so life's frenetic pace
doesn't overtake you like rushing water!

Snoqualmie Falls, Washington © Loretta Woodward Veney, 2016

Write your legacy
through your
great deeds!

Madrid, Spain © Tim Veney, 2016

Getting off the beaten path can lead to beautiful discoveries!

Maui, Hawaii © Loretta Woodward Veney, 2016

Antelope Canyon, Arizona © Tim Veney, 2016

Cherish life's peaks and calm waters and you'll be better prepared when things change.

Skagway, Alaska © Loreta Woodward Veney, 2016

51

There's more than one
way to get up a hill!

Zurich, Switzerland © Tim Veney, 2016

When there is even a glimmer of light, there's hope!

Samana, Dominican Republic © Loretta Veney, 2016

Dubai, United Arab Emirates © Tim Veney, 2016

Copenhagen, Denmark © Tim Veney, 2016

The higher you have to climb, the stronger you get!

Eze, France © Tim Veney, 2016

You see everything more clearly when your spirits are high!

Junfrau, Switzerland © Tim Veney, 2016

Call a friend when you need a lift!

Grand Canyon National Park, Arizona © Tim Veney, 2016

Sometimes we forget that we aren't alone in this world!

Chicago, Illinois © Tim Veney, 2016

Even a few minutes alone can be restorative!

Grand canal, Venice, Italy © Loretta Woodward Veney, 2016

Leave no stone unturned
until you have what you need!

Kodachrome Basin, Utah © Loretta Woodward Veney, 2016

When a path isn't readily
available create your own!

Vancouver, Canada © Loretta Woodward Veney, 2016

From a lofty perch, you can behold the world!

Lucerne, Switzerland © Loretta Woodward Veney, 2016

Look for the beauty and worth in everything and everyone!

Coronado, California © Loretta Woodward Veney, 2016

Even the rain
can be tranquil!

Maui, Hawaii © Tim Veney, 2016

Leave all your worries in your special place!

Martha's Vineyard, Massachusetts © Loretta Woodward Veney, 2016

Magnificent places boost your spirits!

Yosemite National Park, California © Tim Veney 2016

Uniformity can be comforting!

Mykonos, Greece © Tim Veney, 2016

Examine your current situation
from different vantage points!

Chicago, Illinois © Tim Veney, 2016

With the right resources your challenges sail away!

Porto Santo Stefano, Italy © Tim Veney, 2016

Sometimes we need a little direction!

Martha's Vineyard, Massachusetts © Loretta Woodward Veney, 2016

A little time away can bring a lot of solitude!

Xcaret, Mexico © Loretta Woodward Veney, 2016

Some days you feel like you're falling off a ledge, but at the end of the day you'll still be standing!

Grand Canyon National Park West Rim, Arizona © Tim Veney, 2016

Being close to a force
of nature helps you to
feel your own power!

Niagara Falls, Canada © Tim Veney, 2016

Luxor, Egypt © Tim Veney, 2016

Keep looking until you see the big picture!

Copenhagen, Denmark © Loretta Woodward Veney, 2016

Storms may be scary but they always pass!

Moab, Utah © Tim Veney, 2016

Paris, France © Loretta Woodward Veney, 2016

Don't look back, the strong support behind you will hold you up!

Cairo, Egypt © Loretta Woodward Veney, 2016

Life is short, so enjoy a piece of cake or pie!

Pastry shop, Lucca, Italy © Tim Veney, 2016

Greet every morning with the joy of being alive!

Sunrise at Abu Simbel, Egypt © Tim Veney, 2016

Life is tougher without the right pillars in your life!

Athens, Greece © Tim Veney, 2016

Take a quick break to do something fun!

Herkimer, New York © Loretta Woodward Veney, 2016

Exploring different places to dine and shop brings new excitement!

Eze, France © Loretta Woodward Veney, 2016

Get out of the house, you may discover hidden gems!

Nice, France © Loretta Woodward Veney, 2016

Glacier Bay National Park, Alaska © Loretta Woodward Veney, 2016

When you're at your wits end, imagine having a beach all to yourself!

St. Croix, U.S. Virgin Islands, © Loretta Woodward Veney, 2016

You're in charge of your own palace,
don't let others overrule you!

Monaco, France © Tim Veney, 2016

Take life one step at a time
so you don't slip and fall!

Mendenhall Glacier, Alaska © Loretta Woodward Veney, 2016

Encourage the negative people in your life to fly away!

Dubai, United Arab Emirates, © Loretta Woodward Veney, 2016

Your true friends stick with you through thick and thin!

Bryce Canyon, Utah © Loretta Woodward Veney, 2016

Don't miss the rainbows in your life!

Niagara Falls, Canada © Tim Veney, 2016

Lower Antelope Canyon, Arizona © Tim Veney, 2016

Having great relationships includes
building bridges with loved ones.

Natural Bridge, Virginia © Loretta Woodward Veney, 2016

Some days can be
a real bear, but it
will be over soon!

Skyline Drive, Virginia © Loretta Woodward Veney, 2016

Beautiful skies tell a very spiritual story!

La Jolla, California © Tim Veney, 2016

Moments are more precious when you're not watching the clock!

Prague, Czech Republic © Loretta Woodward Veney, 2016

Don't give up even if the path seems impenetrable.

Road to Bryce Canyon, Utah © Loretta Woodward Veney, 2016

It's ok to lean a little when you
don't feel like standing up straight!

Pisa, Italy © Loretta Woodward Veney, 2016

Caring for yourself first ensures continued growth!

Butchart Gardens, Victoria British Columbia, Canada © Tim Veney, 2016

Don't go off in too many directions
or you may end up all wet!

Seattle, Washington, © Tim Veney, 2016

A sanctuary is wherever you feel peace!

Shrine Mont, Orkney Springs, Virginia © Loretta Woodward Veney, 2016

Be a pillar of hope in your community!

Toledo, Spain © Loretta Woodward Veney, 2016

When someone is down, lift them up!

Salzburg, Austria, © Tim Veney, 2016

Your spirit can soar when you take a retreat!

Jungfrau, Switzerland, Tim Veney, 2016

Not even a
huge barrier
should crush
your spirit.

Arches National Park, Utah © Tim Veney, 2016

Strive to make the right moves every day!

Cancun, Mexico © Loretta Woodward Veney, 2016

Wisdom
is the
result of
years of
growth!

Mt. Rainier National Park, Washington © Loretta Woodward Veney, 2016

Opening
closed doors
may reveal
the answers
you need!

Madrid, Spain © Tim Veney, 2016

Make your home your sanctuary!

Maple Valley, Washington © Tim Veney, 2016

Step into a quiet place when you need one!

La Jolla, California © Loretta Woodward Veney, 2016

Take a stroll that makes you feel alive!

Clevedale Historic Inn and Gardens, Spartanburg, South Carolina © Loretta Woodward Veney, 2016

What you believe you're experiencing
may only be an illusion!

Vancouver, Canada © Loretta Woodward Veney, 2016

Don't be so preoccupied that you miss the beautiful things in this world!

Butchart Gardens, Victoria British Columbia, Canada © Tim Veney, 2016

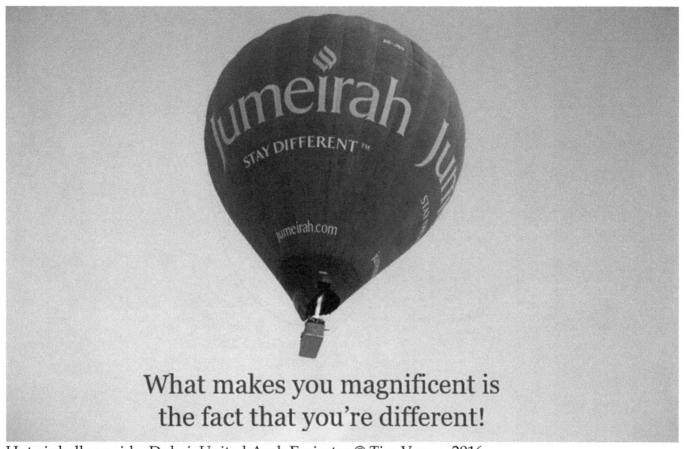

What makes you magnificent is
the fact that you're different!

Hot air balloon ride, Dubai, United Arab Emirates © Tim Veney, 2016

Believe that you are a mighty fortress!

San Juan, Puerto Rico © Loretta Woodward Veney, 2016

Life is short don't let that ship sail without you!

St. Thomas, U.S. Virgin Islands © Loretta Woodward Veney, 2016

Find an energizing outlet so stress doesn't box you in!

Aswan, Egypt © Tim Veney, 2016

Life may twist you around but it won't break you!

Arches National Park, Utah © Loretta Woodward Veney, 2016

Make a wish, it may just come true!

Trevi Fountain, Rome, Italy © Tim Veney, 2016

Valley of the Kings, Luxor, Egypt © Tim Veney, 2016

Discover the sheer joy of being outdoors!

Road to Hana, Maui, Hawaii © Tim Veney, 2016

To really understand a situation, examine it closely!

Scottsdale, Arizona © Loretta Woodward Veney, 2016

Just because the handwriting is on the wall doesn't mean life is over!

Kom Ombo, Egypt © Tim Veney, 2016

When you work on your physical strength
your spiritual strength grows too!

Mt Rainier National Park, Washington © Tim Veney, 2016

Find that special jolt of energy you need!

St. Thomas, U.S. Virgin Islands © Tim Veney, 2016

When you fit all the right pieces together you'll be unstoppable!

Burj Khalifa in Dubai, United Arab Emirates © Tim Veney, 2016

The three greatest pillars of support
are your family, friends and faith!

Pyramids in Cairo, Egypt © Tim Veney, 2016

Let a beautiful environment engulf you!

Herkimer, New York © Loretta Woodward Veney, 2016

Stay calm and work to get to the root of the problem!

Yosemite National Park, California © Loretta Woodward Veney, 2016

When all else fails, gelato may be the answer!

Gelato shop Siena, Italy © Loretta Woodward Veney, 2016

On the toughest days, even a small accomplishment can be a triumph!

Arc de Triomphe, Paris © Loretta Woodward Veney, 2016

Seize the energy each seasonal change brings!

Shenandoah National Park, Virginia © Tim Veney, 2016

When you dance with your
friends, your stress disappears!

Luau in Maui, Hawaii © Tim Veney, 2016

If you're buried under stress, find the resources needed to dig yourself out!

Clinton, Maryland © Loretta Woodward Veney, 2016

You never outgrow
playing in a treehouse!

Herkimer, New York © Loretta Woodward Veney, 2016

Self-care includes enjoying new explorations!

Maui, Hawaii © Tim Veney, 2016

We all need an angel in our lives!

National Harbor's ICE, Washington, D.C. © Tm Veney, 2016

Seek out places that fill you with the spirit!

The Vatican, Rome, Italy © Loretta Woodward Veney, 2016

Antelope Canyon, Arizona © Tim Veney, 2016

Never let the sun
set on your spirit!
Keep moving forward!

Porto Santo Stefano, Italy © Tim Veney, 2016

Nice, France © Loretta Woodward Veney, 2019

The curves life throws at us make us well rounded!

Jordan Pond, Bar Harbor, Maine © Loretta Woodward Veney, 2019

The cookie-cutter approach rarely works,
find the approach that brings comfort!

Scottsdale, Arizona © Loretta Woodward Veney, 2019

Bar Harbor, Maine © Loretta Woodward Veney, 2019

Clevedale Historic Inn and Gardens, Spartanburg, South Carolina © Tim Veney, 2016

Bar Harbor, Maine © Loretta Woodward Veney, 2019

Lancaster, Pennsylvania © Loretta Woodward Veney, 2019

Even the rocky times in our lives seem better when we watch the sun rise!

Brooklin, Maine © Loretta Woodward Veney, 2019

Green grass, plus blue skies and clear water equals tranquility!

Snow Island, Maine © Loretta Woodward Veney, 2019

Taking a stroll along a river can help you catch your breath!

Owego, New York © Loretta Woodward Veney, 2019

Trust your gut to point
you in the right direction!

Aswan, Egypt © Tim Veney 2016

You may find a healthy snack
if you go out for a walk!

Corfu, Greece © Tim Veney 2016

You never know where you'll find an amazing waterfall!

Greenville, South Carolina © Loretta Woodward Veney, 2019

You never know where you may find
a reliable shelter, just keep looking!

Smithsonian exhibit Washington, D.C. © Loretta Woodward Veney, 2019

Getting out for a walk can have a
monumental impact on your spirit!

Washington, D.C. © Loretta Woodward Veney, 2019

A strong and supportive bridge can keep us from falling into troubled waters!

New York City, New York © Loretta Woodward Veney, 2019

Dining in nature is
nourishment for the soul!

St. Paul, Minnesota © Loretta Woodward Veney, 2019

Sunflowers and butterflies
can brighten any day!

Serenity Farm Sunflower Festival, Benedict, Md © Loretta Woodward Veney, 2019

A secluded table may be the
only medicine you need!

Hughesville, MD © Loretta Woodward Veney, 2019

Work Hard
Play Hard
Care Hard

Loretta Woodward Veney

Epilogue

As I look back on all the travel and camping adventures Tim and I experienced in our almost 31 years of marriage, I'm so grateful for both the memories we made and the amazing photos we took to preserve them.

Cherish your family memories!

Contact Information

Want to book Loretta for a speaking engagement?
Loretta Woodward Veney
www.lorettaveney.com
lwveney@lorettaveney.com

Throughout her life, Loretta Woodward Veney, author of *Being My Mom's Mom* and *Colors Flowing from My Mind* has chronicled family events through journals, photos, and videos, seeking to capture every moment. After receiving the devastating news in 2006 that her beloved mother Doris was the first female in the family to suffer from dementia, Loretta began documenting the details of doctor visits, and recording people, places, and things as a substitute for her Mom's lost memory.

Loretta is a motivational speaker and trainer who has delivered more than 300 speeches and presentations on dementia and caregiving since 2014 and she offers a wealth of information and encouragement for her audiences. Loretta and her Mom been featured in articles in the Washington Post, the NY Times and AARP and appeared in a PBS special featuring Alzheimer's Caregivers.

CPSIA information can be obtained
at www.ICGtesting.com
Printed in the USA
JSHW031145280521
15298JS00001B/1